Secret in the Swamp

backpack mysteries

Too Many Treasures
Big Island Search
Phantom Gardener
Twin Trouble
Secret in the Swamp
Rock Patrol

9705

a backpack Mystery

Secret in the Swamp

Mary Carpenter Reid

BETHANY HOUSE PUBLISHERS
MINNEAPOLIS, MINNESOTA 55438

Published by Bethany House Publishers
A Ministry of Bethany Fellowship, Inc.
11300 Hampshire Avenue South
Minneapolis, Minnesota 55438

Printed in the United States of America.

Library of Congress Cataloging-in-Publication Data

Reid, Mary.
    Secret in the swamp / by Mary Carpenter Reid.
        p.   cm. — (A backpack mystery ; 5)
    Summary: Steff and her younger sister Paulie look for clues to the whereabouts of their uncle's missing noteboook which contains valuable research on swamps.
    ISBN 1–55661–719–4 (pbk.)
    [1. Swamps—Fiction. 2. Sisters—Fiction. 3. Christian life—Fiction. 4. Mystery and detective stories.] I. Title. II. Series: Reid, Mary. Backpack mystery ; 5.
PZ7.R2727Se   1997
[Fic]—dc21   97–21038
                                             CIP
                                              AC

To a fellow in my family
named Frank.

MARY CARPENTER REID loves to visit places just like the places Steff and Paulie visit. Does she stay with peculiar relatives? That's her secret!

She will tell you her family is wonderful. She likes reading and writing children's books. She likes colors and computers. She especially likes getting letters from her readers.

She can't organize things as well as Steff does, but she makes lots of lists.

Two cats—a calico and a tiger cat—live at her house in California. *They* are very peculiar!

Contents

1. Sticky Notes 9
2. The Lost Notebook 13
3. Zigzag Tag 18
4. Rumors of Treasure 26
5. Something Hidden 31
6. The Earth Is Moving...................... 34
7. Rummage Sale 38
8. A Visit to the Sheriff..................... 43
9. Saturday Deadline 48
10. Gone for Good 52
11. Paulie's Knees 56
12. At Trail's End 60
13. Look in the Canoe 63
14. Start Explaining! 69
15. Beulah's Secret 73

Let the word of Christ dwell in you richly. . . .

Colossians 3:16

Sticky Notes

Scrape! Slide! Crash!

Steff Larson bolted up in bed.

From somewhere came sounds of tumbling metal and breaking glass. A motor howled. A thundering *BOOM!* made her heart pound. She shook herself awake. "Whew!" she breathed as she decided those scary noises were far away.

Here in this pretty upstairs bedroom, morning sun peeped through ruffled curtains. It shone on her backpack hanging from a chair.

But this was not her room. "Where. . . ?"

Then she remembered her parents driving her and Paulie to this small southern town the day before. She remembered Uncle Theodore and Aunt Wilma and this white house with the porch on three sides.

She remembered telling Paulie, "Don't cry. Mom and Dad have to go to the trade show. It helps our business. They will come get us in four days."

Now Steff looked toward her younger sister's bed.

Paulie's brown eyes peeked over the white sheet. "What's making that noise?"

Steff grinned because she'd figured it out. "A trash truck—the kind that picks up giant trash containers and empties them."

A peculiar, deep cry bellowed through the air.

That was no trash truck!

Steff crept to the window.

Below lay a big backyard and a peach orchard. Somewhere beyond that lay the entrance to a huge swamp.

A man walked in the yard, looking at the

ground. Sun glinted on top of his shiny head.

Steff called, "Uncle Theodore, what's that noise?"

"A trash truck over at the swamp."

"The other noise."

"Oh, you mean Earl." Uncle Theodore peeled a small square of paper off a wooden lawn chair. It looked like a sticky note. "Earl always sings with the trash truck."

Paulie squeezed next to Steff at the window. "Earl who?"

Uncle Theodore held his brown-rimmed glasses in place and peered under the chair. "You'll meet Earl."

Steff asked, "Did you lose something?"

"I'm afraid I did—an important notebook." He walked toward the back door. "Come down for breakfast soon."

On the dresser were pads of sticky notes.

Steff handed a bunch to Paulie. "Uncle Theodore said these were for us. Put them in your backpack."

"What for?"

"To write down things. Or to mark pages in

our school books. Mom asked Uncle Theodore to help us with our lessons. He uses sticky notes everywhere."

"I know." Paulie rolled her eyes. "Even on the lawn chair, and in the bathroom above our towels, and—"

"Paulie," Steff stopped her. "Just think about sticky notes. Think of all the great ways you could use them to sort things and organize stuff."

Paulie sighed. "Here we go again. You always want to organize everything."

Steff flipped her thumb across the edge of a yellow pad. The pages fluttered with a soft purring sound. She smiled. "Why, I could organize almost anything with sticky notes."

2

the Lost Notebook

At the kitchen table, the girls found pink sticky notes in their cereal bowls. Bible verses were written on the notes.

Steff read hers aloud. "'Let the word of Christ dwell in you richly'. . . . Colossians 3:16."

Uncle Theodore passed the cereal. "Use the notes to help you memorize the verses. We'll have a new verse tomorrow."

Paulie stuck hers on her shirt.

Uncle Theodore said, "Never stop memorizing Scripture. If you hide God's Word in your heart, it will be there when you need it."

Aunt Wilma came in and hugged both girls. "How are my darlings this morning?"

Aunt Wilma worked in a beauty shop and fixed people's hair. Yesterday, her own hair was pretty—puffed up high, with smooth curls all over.

But this morning, her hair was squashed flat, except for loose strands that stuck up on top like dry weeds.

Paulie stared as Aunt Wilma put bread in the toaster.

Steff knew her sister was getting ready to say something awful.

She did. "What color is your hair, Aunt Wilma?"

Aunt Wilma didn't seem to mind. "Blond, number 920—it says on the bottle. I add a little number 957 to that for puh-zazz."

"Does the puh-zazz make your hair pink?"

Uncle Theodore coughed into his napkin.

Aunt Wilma whacked him on the back as if he might be choking.

Paulie pulled her own brown hair where she could see it. "I wonder what number my hair is."

Steff wanted to groan. Sometimes Paulie was such a child.

Aunt Wilma looked at a paper on the refrigerator door. "Your parents are working at the trade show all day. They'll probably call you tonight."

Steff hoped so.

"When can we go to the swamp?" asked Paulie.

Uncle Theodore said, "After breakfast." He took a memo book from his shirt pocket and opened it. Sticky notes clung to the pages. "Let me see . . . I'm giving a talk to a fourth-grade class this morning in the museum auditorium."

Aunt Wilma poured coffee. "Theodore, did you find your research notebook yet?"

"No."

She told the girls, "Your uncle has a problem. He lost a notebook. It's thin, like this." She held her thumb and finger close together. "It is filled with important information.

He needs to find it by Saturday so he can finish writing some kind of book."

"That *some kind of book*," Uncle Theodore said, "is a history of human habitation of the swamp."

Aunt Wilma winked. "He means people who lived in the swamp."

Uncle Theodore closed his memo book. A sticky note was left on the table. He tucked it under his watchband. "All the money earned from selling my book will be used to pay for new displays at the swamp museum."

"What color is your notebook?" asked Steff.

Uncle Theodore glared at his wife. "Pink, mostly."

Aunt Wilma raised her eyebrows. "The cover *was* a dull gray until I painted pink flowers—petunias—on it with nail polish. It looked much better when I finished."

Uncle Theodore said, "Not everyone would agree, Wilma. Anyway, the notebook is lost. I haven't seen it since yesterday morning."

"What happens if you don't find it?" asked Steff.

He frowned. "I'm in trouble. It contains all the information I have on a certain family that lived in the swamp about seventy years ago. They had a girl named Beulah. Without the missing research notebook, I can't write the story of Beulah's family."

Paulie said, "Steff and I will find your notebook."

"How sweet," cooed Aunt Wilma.

"Oh, I mean it," said Paulie. "We *really* will find it. Steff will make a plan. She is good at that."

Steff thought to herself that Paulie was good at making promises. Still, how hard could it be to find a dull gray notebook painted with pink petunias—especially if she organized the search using sticky notes?

"Yes," she said. "Paulie and I will find your notebook."

3

zigzag tag

The entrance to the swamp looked like a park. Water flowed in streams wide enough for small boats. Flowers bloomed. Sidewalks led over bridges and around the lawn to the museum and other buildings.

"I thought the swamp would be wild and lonely," Paulie told Uncle Theodore.

"I thought it would be a big, muddy lake," said Steff.

"This is only a tiny part of the swamp," Uncle Theodore said. "Much of the rest is wild and lonely, and much of it does look like a lake. All the water is quite clear. See?" He scooped some into his hands. "That's because it flows very slowly."

Paulie stuck her finger in it. "Looks a little brown."

"Something called tannic acid makes the water this color. We say it's tea-colored."

Uncle Theodore called to a tall man wearing a blue hat. On the hat was written *Al's Boats*. Above that was a drawing of a funny little alligator driving a boat.

Uncle Theodore told the girls, "Mr. Allen runs Al's Boathouse here at the swamp."

While the men talked, Steff and Paulie went over to a stream.

Paulie threw a stick across the water to the other side.

She squealed. "You try it, Steff. Try to hit that log on the bank."

Steff reached for a stick at the edge of the water. It wouldn't move. She tugged hard— harder—harder! The stick cracked and came loose. She lost her balance and slid down the bank.

Paulie shouted, "Help! Somebody help!"

"I'm OK!" Steff cried. She sprawled on the bank, her feet splashing the water.

Suddenly, someone grabbed her hands from behind and started pulling her up the bank. "Stop kicking the water!" a strange voice ordered.

Steff tilted her head back and saw a tall boy above her. He hung on to her hands and kept pulling.

She felt dumb, dumb, dumb.

Finally, he let loose.

Steff scrambled to her feet and wiped her muddy shoes on the grass.

The boy said, "Take a good look at that log on the other bank."

Paulie cried, "Steff, it's moving!"

Slowly, the log raised up. One end swung around and pointed toward them.

Steff gasped. The log was not a log. It was a huge alligator.

Only the narrow stream of water ran

between them and the alligator. The alligator seemed big enough and long enough to cross that water with one good push.

Uncle Theodore and Mr. Allen rushed over.

"Don't get that fellow too excited," said Uncle Theodore.

The alligator watched for a minute. Then it turned away and settled back down in the grass.

Steff hissed, "Uncle Theodore, that's an alligator! Right there! Without a fence or anything!"

"Didn't I say you would meet Earl?"

Mr. Allen chuckled. "You probably heard him bellowing this morning when the trash truck came."

"But he's so—so big, and he's so close!" said Steff. "Shouldn't he be in a cage?"

"Oh, we don't worry much about Earl," said Uncle Theodore. "He gets plenty to eat."

"Eat? Like what?" Paulie clung to Uncle Theodore's arm.

"We make sure the alligators that hang around here at the entrance get meat. However, out on his own, Earl would eat about anything that moves."

Paulie stood perfectly still. She gulped. "Anything that moves?"

"Well, he would have to catch it first," said Uncle Theodore.

The tall boy grinned. He wore a blue hat like Mr. Allen's. "Alligators can swim fast and run fast. But they cannot turn quickly. So if you are ever chased by an alligator, run in a zigzag line."

He darted across the grass, turning sharply first to one side and then the other. "See?" He came back laughing.

Steff still felt dumb about being dragged away from the water. She said, "I suppose you call that zigzag tag?" Then she felt even more dumb.

Mr. Allen told the girls, "This is my son, Russell. Come to our boathouse this afternoon. He'll take you for a ride."

Uncle Theodore said, "Russell is only sixteen, but he's a real tour guide."

"Cool!" said Paulie. "Except"—she looked

worried—"I hope we don't meet any more alligators."

The girls and Uncle Theodore went to the swamp museum. A sign on the door read *Closed*.

Uncle Theodore unlocked the door.

Inside the dark museum, the only light came from a small, high window.

"Now, where's that light switch?" Uncle Theodore muttered.

Steff walked forward. Suddenly, above her face, there appeared an open mouth, longer than her arm and filled with ugly teeth.

"Alligator!" Paulie squawked.

The girls whirled and ran for the door, smacking into Uncle Theodore.

"Oof!" he groaned.

The lights clicked on.

Uncle Theodore was backed against the wall, his hand on the light switch. His books and papers lay scattered on the floor. A green sticky note dangled from his glasses.

He caught his breath. "Don't worry! It's only Winston." He chuckled. "For being a stuffed alligator, Winston does look fierce."

"Yes!" said Steff. "And alive!"

The alligator on display was awesome. It was twelve feet long, with skin that looked like a slightly used tire.

"Uh-oh!" Paulie pointed to the ugly teeth. "I guess Winston didn't brush twice a day."

"Or floss," said Steff.

The door rattled. A man with curly black hair opened it. He seemed surprised to find anyone there.

Uncle Theodore said firmly, "Young man, the museum is not open to visitors now."

The man walked on in. "Oh, I just want to look around."

But Uncle Theodore stepped in front of him and repeated, "The museum is not open."

The man carried a large bag. He swung the strap up to one shoulder and stood there scowling. Finally, he turned and went outside.

Steff wondered how anyone could have missed seeing the closed sign on the museum door.

4

rumors of treasure

"Who was that?" asked Steff.

Uncle Theodore sat down on a bench and wiped his head with a handkerchief. "He says his name is Nick. He's been hanging around the last few days. He was recording my talks to visitors with his video camera, until I told him to stop."

"He didn't seem very nice," said Paulie.

"The problem is, I'm afraid he may not be honest. I'm worried he might put the stories I tell in a film that he will sell."

"Like a nature film for television?" asked Steff.

"Yes. I've spent many years learning about the swamp and the people who lived here. Now that I no longer teach school, I'm writing my stories in the book I told you about. I want that swamp book to be sold to make money for this museum. I don't want my stories to make money for that man."

Uncle Theodore slapped his knee. "Well, let's hope Nick is not trying to steal my stories. Let's hope he is simply a curious person."

The girls helped Uncle Theodore look in his office for the missing notebook. The room was crowded with books and papers. Sticky notes climbed the walls.

Thin gray research notebooks filled several shelves. Each notebook had a little frame on the front cover, with a white card slipped inside the frame. On the card was written Uncle Theodore's last name, *Newton*.

Steff wrote *Card—Newton* on a sticky note. She stuck it in a small purple record book. "A clue to help find the missing notebook," she told Paulie.

Uncle Theodore put on a badge. It read *Docent*.

"Is that your middle name?" asked Paulie.

He chuckled. "No. It's a fancy word for volunteer. I work here almost every day, and I don't get a paycheck."

Paulie said, "After our dad was laid off from his job, he didn't get a paycheck."

"That's why he and Mom started our business," said Steff.

Paulie mumbled, "But now they always have to go on trips."

Steff said, "Only when it's important for the business, Paulie."

Uncle Theodore said, "Well, your Aunt Wilma and I are glad you can stay with us."

Soon it was time for Uncle Theodore to talk to the fourth graders in the auditorium.

He told them of a logging company that came to the swamp. The workers cut cypress trees and moved them out on a railroad. He told of a large island in the swamp called Sneezeweed Island.

"On the island was a town where the workers lived with their families," said Uncle Theodore. "The town had a school and church and stores. When the logging stopped about seventy years ago, everyone was out of a job. The workers moved away. Today, there is nothing left of the town."

Then Uncle Theodore asked for questions.

Someone spoke from the back of the auditorium. "Sir?"

Steff looked around. It was Nick.

Uncle Theodore called on the fourth graders who held up their hands.

Nick kept saying, "Sir? Sir?"

Finally, Uncle Theodore pointed to him.

Nick asked, "Can you talk about the rich families that lived in the swamp? You know, every swamp has rumors of hidden treasure."

Uncle Theodore answered, "Treasure? I'm sure any talk of treasure would be only a rumor." He quickly pointed to the clock. "Time is up for today."

Steff looked again. Nick was gone.

5

Something Hidden

The girls and Uncle Theodore started home for lunch. Visitors crowded the sidewalk.

Steff said, "Tell us about Beulah, the girl in your missing notebook."

Uncle Theodore said, "Beulah's family lived in the swamp, but not in the logging town where most people lived. She walked to town for school and for church. I remember that her name was on the church records of people who were baptized."

Steff liked hearing that Beulah had been baptized.

"Was Beulah's family rich?" asked Paulie.

"Probably not," Uncle Theodore said. "They moved away about the same time all the people left the logging town. I believe Beulah was twelve years old then. I talked to a woman who said Beulah wrote her one letter after that. In that letter, Beulah said she was ill on moving day. She had to leave behind something important—something that she had hidden."

"A treasure is important," said Paulie.

"Paulie," Steff said, "if Beulah had hidden a lot of money, she would have told her parents. They would have gotten it for her on moving day."

"I never saw Beulah's letter," said Uncle Theodore. "That story of leaving something important behind could be wrong."

"Will your swamp book be the true story?" asked Steff.

"As true as I can make it," Uncle Theodore said. "For many years, I studied old records and newspapers. Also, I talked to everyone I could find who knew about people who lived in the swamp. I wrote down what those people said. I put everything in my research notebooks. I'm using those notebooks to write my swamp book."

"But your Beulah notebook is missing," said Paulie.

Steff asked, "Can you get the stuff about Beulah again?"

"No. There is not enough time. Besides, the people I found who remembered Beulah's family are no longer living." Uncle Theodore shook his head sadly. "No, I can never replace what is in my Beulah notebook."

"Ouch!" Paulie cried. "There's a rock in my shoe." She limped over to the grass and plopped down.

Nearby stood a man with black curly hair. Steff could not see his face. Hanging over his back was a video camera.

The camera pointed at the ground, but a small red light glowed. That meant the camera was turned on. It could be recording their voices.

Steff showed Uncle Theodore.

He frowned, then whispered cheerfully, "Glad we weren't telling secrets."

But Steff knew her uncle was not really cheerful.

6

the earth is moving

Late that afternoon, Uncle Theodore went to a meeting. The girls went to Al's Boathouse.

The open, flat boats looked like rowboats, except they had motors at the back. About nine people climbed out of one.

"Old Earl could probably jump right in those boats," said Paulie.

Russell said, "Nah! Earl knows he can't ride without a ticket." Russell untied a boat. "Come on. My dad says you girls don't need tickets."

He headed the boat along a stream away from the entrance.

The sun beat down. Steff's clothes felt damp.

Russell stopped the boat near a grassy bank and hopped out. "Watch this!" He began to jump up and down on the bank.

Steff teased, "Is that some kind of southern trampoline?"

"Sort of!" Russell said.

Water sloshed. The boat rocked.

"See?" he called. "The earth is moving!"

Steff opened her mouth to tell him he was strange.

But she saw that the earth where Russell was jumping was indeed rising and falling.

"What is going on?" demanded Steff.

Russell climbed back into the boat. The ground settled down and looked like any other ground.

"This is called a peat bed," Russell said. "It used to be rotting leaves and plants on the bottom of the swamp. Large chunks of this stuff float up to the top. Grass begins to grow on it. Seeds fall on it and sprout. A peat bed is a floating mass of roots—and fun to jump on."

Paulie leaned over and fluttered her fingers in the cool tea-colored water. "It doesn't look like anything is rotting down there."

Steff lifted a handful of water to her nose. "It smells fine." She threw the water at Paulie. "Here, you smell it."

Paulie squealed and scooped water at Steff.

Russell backed the boat away. They passed fallen logs and stumps with strange shapes. Ahead, the water lay still and shiny like a mirror, making it hard to tell where the water ended and the land began. A great blue heron flew overhead. Steff was sure animals could be watching from the bank.

Paulie said, "Russell, we heard about treasure hidden in the swamp."

"Sure! Everybody thinks there's treasure in the swamp."

Paulie said, "Don't laugh. My uncle has a notebook full of stuff about a girl named Beulah. She moved away and left something important in the swamp."

Steff gave Paulie a stern look. "You don't know that Beulah left any treasure."

Then she told Russell, "My uncle's notebook is what's important. It is missing, and he needs to find it right away. The cover is gray with pink petunias."

"Petunias? Are you kidding?"

"No," Steff told him.

Russell shook his head. "Haven't seen it."

They neared the boathouse. Standing on the dock was a man with black curly hair.

Russell said, "But I do keep seeing that guy with the video camera."

7

rummage sale

The next morning, Steff read from a blue sticky note on her juice glass, " 'The Lord watches over you'. . . . Psalm 121:5." That would be easy to memorize.

"Remember," said Uncle Theodore, "the sticky notes are only reminders to help you learn the verse."

After breakfast, the girls worked on math and spelling.

Later, they walked downtown with Uncle Theodore.

He stopped outside the town library. He pointed to the next corner. "That's our church. See the ice cream shop across from it?" He took bills from his wallet. "You girls get yourselves some ice cream while I go to the library."

At the ice cream shop, Steff told Paulie, "We're in the south. I'm getting a southern flavor. Peach Fuzz Freeze."

"Ugh!"

"You can have Pecan Butter Brickle. Or Peanut Power. Or Watermelon Squish. Or . . ."

Paulie made a face at Steff. She told the server, "I'd like a Double Chocolate Trouble, please. Large."

They carried their cones outside and sat on a bench.

Paulie's Double Chocolate Trouble began to melt in the hot sun. Brown drips rolled down her arms.

Steff scooted away. "Don't get chocolate on me."

Paulie licked faster. "Look at yourself— Peach Fuzz Freeze face."

Uncle Theodore's church across the street

was red brick with white columns. Two huge trees shaded a green lawn. Between the trees hung a banner that read *Rummage Sale*.

"Let's go over there in the shade," said Steff.

At the sale, Paulie saw something she wanted. "Oh! Look at this tin box with swirls on top. I could keep my jewelry in here."

"Do you have any money?"

Paulie held out two quarters smeared with Double Chocolate Trouble.

"That is change from the ice cream. It belongs to Uncle Theodore."

"Did you bring money? I'll pay you back. This is the most beautiful tin box in the whole world."

Steff sighed. "Let's look around before we decide on anything."

"Aha! You *did* bring money. How much?"

"A little."

Steff saw a box of books. She gulped down the last of her ice-cream cone and wiped her hands with a napkin.

Between two books was a wrinkled paper. She held it up. It was old and dirty.

Steff read the words at the top. " 'My Secret.' "

"It's a poem," said Paulie.

"Yes—written in the olden days."

"What's that word at the bottom?"

Steff squinted. "It says Beulah!" She gasped. "It must be Uncle Theodore's Beulah! She wrote this very poem."

The girls were studying the paper when Steff heard a woman say, "Sorry, I didn't mean to walk in front of your camera."

Steff turned. A man holding a video camera ducked behind a tree.

Steff suddenly felt cold—colder than Peach Fuzz Freeze.

The man with the camera was Nick.

Steff was sure he had been pointing his camera at her and Paulie.

a visit to the sheriff

Steff grabbed Paulie and rushed to the lady taking money.

She asked, "How much for this paper?"

The woman said, "My! There's no price marked."

Steff looked for Nick. "Would a dollar be enough?"

Paulie hissed, "You had a whole dollar?"

The woman said, "I think ten cents is a fair price." She gave Steff change.

Paulie asked her sister, "Can I borrow fifty

cents to buy the tin box? I'll pay you back."

Steff dragged her across the lawn. "Come on!"

"What's your hurry?" Paulie pulled away and picked up the tin box.

"Pauline Larson!" Steff growled. "Nick is here. He was taking a video of us."

Paulie's mouth fell open. "Oh! I see him. He's talking to the woman who sold us the poem."

She dropped the tin box, and the girls ran to the library.

Inside, they found Uncle Theodore. A line of green sticky notes marched across the table where he sat.

Steff slid the paper in front of him. "We bought this poem at the rummage sale. Beulah wrote it."

Paulie said, "It's called 'My Secret.' Listen to the first two lines.

While taking a dip in a cup of tea,
A glorious treasure came to me.

That means Beulah really did have a treasure."

Uncle Theodore exclaimed, "I don't know about a treasure, but this poem is quite a find! She might have written it for school."

Paulie said, "Now you can finish your swamp book."

"I'm afraid I still need my research notebook."

Steff plopped in a chair. Finding the poem hadn't been as important as she'd thought.

Paulie propped her chin in her hands. "I wonder why Nick was taking a video of us at the rummage sale."

"What?" Uncle Theodore barked.

A woman glared. "Shhh!"

The girls quietly told him about seeing Nick.

He peeled his sticky notes from the table. "Come on. I'm going to talk to the sheriff about that guy."

When Uncle Theodore came out of the sheriff's office, he said, "The librarian already complained about Nick. He kept bothering her, asking to see old records about people who once lived in the swamp. The sheriff is keeping an eye on him."

Paulie exclaimed, "We were right! He *is* making a film on the swamp. He's going to sell it for a lot of money."

Steff told Uncle Theodore, "He'd better not be copying your stories."

Paulie exclaimed, "That would be cheating!"

Uncle Theodore said firmly, "It's also called plagiarism!"

"Play . . . what?" Paulie frowned.

Uncle Theodore explained, "Plagiarism means taking someone else's work and pretending it is your own."

Paulie sounded out the word, "*Play-jer-ism.*"

Uncle Theodore nodded. "Yes, and you're right. A plagiarist is a cheater."

At home, Steff studied Beulah's poem. "Listen to this line.

A garden grows, a rooster crows.

I think she was writing about where she lived."

Paulie told Uncle Theodore, "You said Beulah walked to school and church. She must have lived close to the logging town."

"Let's go look for her house," said Steff.

"By now, it might be only a pile of rotting boards," Uncle Theodore warned.

Paulie said, "Let me see that line about her treasure.

It waits inside a house of glass.

What does that mean?"

Steff shrugged. "Maybe a house with many windows?"

Saturday deadline

After lunch, the phone rang. Uncle Theodore hung it up with a sigh. "Bad news. I asked for more time to finish writing my book. The answer is no. I still must find my research notebook by Saturday."

"Find notebook—Saturday," Steff said. "Paulie, put that on a yellow sticky note."

"I don't need to. I can remember Saturday."

Steff said, "How can we expect to find anything if we aren't organized?"

Later, the girls went to Al's Boathouse while

Uncle Theodore went to the museum.

Steff showed Beulah's poem to Russell. "We want to find her house. Listen to this line.

By cypress knees where trees once rose.

Do you know any place like that?"

"Sure."

"Would you take us there?"

Russell shook his head. "I can't."

"Why?"

"I can't take you *every* place that trees once rose. People talk about roots of cypress trees having knees. Beulah could have been writing about the stumps left after the trees were cut. Thousands of trees were cut when the loggers worked here. Sorry."

"OK." Steff sighed. "Come on, Paulie. Let's go to the museum."

The girls passed the stream where they'd first met Earl.

Paulie grabbed Steff's arm. "Look. He's there!"

"Earl?"

"No," Paulie said. "Nick—standing near the

museum. He's probably trying to record Uncle Theodore's talk."

"Cheat!"

"Plager!"

"That's plagiarist," Steff corrected her. "*Play-jer-ist.*"

Nick saw them watching. He quickly walked away.

Outside the museum, Steff picked up a small white card. On it was written *Newton*.

Paulie squealed, "Look! There's pink on one corner—like pink petunias."

"Well!" exclaimed Steff. "Isn't it odd that this card just happened to be on the ground right where that cheating Nick was standing?"

"Yes," Paulie nodded wisely. "As if it fell off the front cover of something he was holding."

"That something is a gray notebook with pink petunias. Nick must have Uncle Theodore's missing notebook."

Uncle Theodore came out of the museum. The girls rushed to show him the card.

He rubbed his thumb over the speck of pink. "You know, girls, that pink polish your aunt put on my Beulah notebook could have chipped off and gotten on others. I carry around lots of research notebooks. Why, I could have dropped this card myself from one of them. No, I'm afraid this doesn't prove that Nick has my notebook."

Steff felt awful. The search for the missing notebook was not going well. Maybe she should use more sticky notes.

gone for good

The next morning, Aunt Wilma said, "I'm leaving early today to go by the church. I forgot to drop off one bag of things for the rummage sale."

Uncle Theodore handed her a pad of white sticky notes. "Try writing yourself a note."

"I know just what to do with sticky notes." She slapped one on top of his shiny head.

Then she told the girls, "Come to the shop in about an hour. I'll do your nails." She took Paulie's hands in hers. "We'll try Pink Bubbles on you."

Paulie looked at Aunt Wilma's hair. "Is that anything like number 957 puh-zazz?"

Uncle Theodore snickered and ducked into his library.

Later, at the beauty shop, the telephone rang.

Aunt Wilma answered. "Girls, it's your mother. She sounds lonesome for you."

Steff talked first. She told about Earl and the boat ride and how she and Paulie were looking for Uncle Theodore's lost notebook.

Paulie kept jumping up and down wanting her turn. She talked about Earl and Double Chocolate Trouble ice cream.

That afternoon, Steff and Paulie did lessons, memorized Bible verses, and searched for the notebook.

Bits of Beulah's poem kept running through Steff's head.

She looked for the poem.

"Paulie!" she shrieked. "Beulah's poem is not in my backpack."

"What? You lost it?"

Steff thought quickly. "I had it at the beauty

shop! I might have put it down by the telephone."

Just then Aunt Wilma came in the back door. "Hel-loooo! I'm home."

Steff ran to meet her. "Did you find an old, old piece of paper with writing at your shop? Maybe near the telephone?"

Paulie grabbed Aunt Wilma's hand. "Steff lost Beulah's poem! We have to go get it."

"Hold on, sweeties. That shop gets cleaned every single day before I leave. There isn't a hank of hair or an old scrap of paper anywhere."

"You mean somebody threw out Beulah's poem?" cried Steff.

"If that poem was left in the shop, it is gone for good."

11

pɑulie'ſ kNeeſ

Up in her room, Steff tried to remember the poem. She was able to write some lines on yellow sticky notes. She put them in her purple record book.

She said, "Beulah's poem could be full of clues telling where her house is and where the treasure is."

Paulie sat cross-legged on her bed. "Even before you lost the poem, it didn't tell us all that."

"Beulah wanted to talk about her treasure but still keep it secret. Now that I think more about her, I see she was very organized. Probably every word in the poem is important."

Paulie lifted her eyebrows. "Organized? You two could have been best friends."

Steff liked that idea.

Suddenly, she remembered another line.

"At trail's end where people pass."

"OK. It's at the end of a trail," said Paulie. "But what are people passing?" She stuck a pink sticky note on her upper lip and blew at it.

"They're just passing, that's all. Passing along the trail."

"But where does the trail end?"

"At Beulah's house, I suppose."

Paulie rolled her eyes. "We don't know where that is or which trail."

Steff gritted her teeth. Paulie was right, and perhaps there wasn't any trail now.

"Of course," said Paulie, "maybe Beulah didn't mean a walking trail. What about a horse trail or a wagon trail or—"

"A railroad!" squealed Steff. "Uncle

Theodore said the workers took logs out of the swamp on a railroad."

"The poem says at trail's end. Railroads are long. I don't think they ever end."

Steff watched Paulie put pink sticky notes on her ankles and up her legs.

"Paulie, you are wasting sticky notes."

"They're mine."

"You should write things on them."

"I don't have anything to write."

By now, the sticky notes reached Paulie's knees.

"Knees!" Steff shouted. She grabbed a yellow sticky note. "I remember another line—about cypress knees."

They found Uncle Theodore in his library.

Steff told him, "Beulah's house is where the railroad ends. The railroad ends at a place where cypress stumps were left after the trees were cut."

Uncle Theodore studied Steff's yellow sticky notes. He grinned. "I like the way you organize."

He fumbled through papers on his desk

until he found a blue sticky note with a phone number. He dialed the telephone.

Then he told the girls, "Let's take a boat ride to Sneezeweed Island."

12

at trail's end

Russell drove the boat with Uncle Theodore and the girls far into the swamp.

They crossed wide, open water dotted with white water lilies and floating green leaves as big as plates. They entered waterways so narrow that Steff and Paulie touched the brush on both sides. Strands of lacy Spanish moss hung from trees.

Once, Steff thought she saw another boat behind them. But no one else saw it.

Finally, they stopped and tied up their boat. They walked until they reached an old railroad. They followed it a short way. Big cypress trees had once grown here.

Suddenly, the railroad tracks stopped.

Steff took her purple record book out of her backpack and read from sticky notes. "At trail's end where people pass. By cypress knees where trees once rose. This is the place!"

Near the end of the railroad tracks, they saw what was left of a broken-down building. There were no doors. The roof had fallen in. It probably had been a house with three rooms.

"We've found Beulah's home!" shouted Paulie.

Russell discovered a heap of rotting boards that could have been a chicken house.

Paulie pretended to be in the garden. "Look! I'm picking green beans."

Steff climbed a small, strangely shaped hill, a little taller than she. It was bumpy and covered with grass and weeds. At the top, she slipped and slid all the way down.

"Ouch!" She rubbed her leg. "That dirt is hard!"

The girls sat in front of the house.

"It's sad," Steff told Paulie, "to think of Beulah and her family leaving home."

Uncle Theodore said, "We'd better go."

Steff knew he must be disappointed. There wasn't much here to write about in his swamp book.

Paulie said, "We didn't find a treasure yet."

"Look around you," said Uncle Theodore. "This was a simple home. It doesn't seem like a hiding place for treasure."

Steff checked the sticky notes in her purple record book.

Paulie told her, "Sticky notes don't help unless you write the right stuff on them."

Russell started back along the railroad. "We'll cut over to the water and follow it to our boat."

The sun began to set.

Near the water, Russell suddenly stopped.

Steff saw an empty canoe tied to the bank. A man stood on the shore.

How odd to find someone else in this lonely spot.

Then Steff realized it was not odd at all.

The man was Nick. He had followed them into the swamp!

13

Look in the canoe

Nick's bag lay on the ground. He was studying a sheet of paper.

"Hmm," Uncle Theodore said. "I'm going to have a talk with this Nick fellow. I want to know why he sticks closer to us than a sticky note. I want to know why he was taking video pictures of my nieces."

Uncle Theodore walked over to Nick.

As the two men talked, Steff saw something on a seat in Nick's canoe.

She crept closer. Paulie and Russell followed.

"Look in the canoe," Steff whispered. "A gray notebook with pink petunias!"

Paulie squeaked, "Nick has Uncle Theodore's notebook!"

Russell said, "Why, that sneaky thief!"

"Plager!" said Paulie.

"That's plagiarist," Steff told her.

Nick was not watching his canoe.

Steff stared at Uncle Theodore's notebook. She should just go over there and pick it up.

The more she thought about Nick having it, the angrier she became. "I'm going to get that notebook back!" she declared.

Paulie gasped. "How?"

"I'll just run over there behind Nick and grab it."

"You're asking for trouble!" Russell warned.

"I'm coming with you," said Paulie.

Steff didn't stop to plan. She began running.

Paulie followed.

Russell muttered, "Wait for me."

A narrow stream of water flowed between them and the spot of ground where Nick stood.

Steff took a flying leap over the water and

landed behind Nick. So did Paulie and Russell, at almost the same moment.

Steff stepped toward the canoe.

But something was wrong with her legs. She was losing her balance. Her arms flailed.

The ground was moving!

"Hey!" Nick whirled to face them.

Paulie yelled and staggered toward Russell.

Uncle Theodore called, "Careful! You're on a floating peat bed."

The canoe bobbed in the water.

Steff fell on her stomach, her hands on the side of the bouncing canoe. She pulled it close and reached one hand over on the seat. Her fingers touched the notebook.

"What's going on?" Nick hollered.

He couldn't stand up, either. He waved his arms wildly and toppled into the water with a big splash.

The canoe bobbed harder.

But Steff grabbed the notebook and scooted back from the canoe. She got partway up.

Just then Paulie fell against her.

The notebook flew out of Steff's hands and into the water.

"The notebook!" Steff yelled. "It's drowning!"

The pink petunias sank slowly in the tea-colored water.

Russell jumped in, feet first. The water was not deep. He bent over and scooped up the notebook. "Got it!"

His blue hat floated nearby.

Steff was on her hands and knees.

Russell's hat moved farther into the water. He waded toward it.

Steff got a strange feeling—a fearful feeling.

She looked past the floating hat with the logo of a funny little alligator.

Across the water, she saw a real alligator—a big one.

The alligator swung his head toward Russell's hat.

Russell kept wading.

Steff tried to scream a warning. But she was so frightened, her voice wouldn't work.

Please, God, Steff prayed silently. Then into

her mind popped the verse, *"The Lord watches over you. . . ."*

Steff swallowed, took a breath, and yelled, "Alligator! Get back, Russell!"

Start explaining!

Russell turned and dove for the peat bed just as the alligator dove for Russell's hat.

Now everyone was yelling.

Russell pulled himself onto the peat bed.

Nick scrambled up on land, too.

They all hurried far from the water.

Steff and Paulie dropped to the ground and sat as close to their uncle as they could.

Uncle Theodore shook water from his notebook. Pink petunias glowed on its cover. He said, "I'm sure glad to get this back."

Paulie said, "Now you can finish writing your swamp book."

Steff told him, "Uncle Theodore, you were right. If you memorize Bible verses, they will be there when you need them. When I saw that alligator, I thought of the verse we learned yesterday and I wasn't so scared."

Uncle Theodore smiled at her. Then he said, "Nick, start explaining! What were you doing with my notebook?"

"I bought it at the church rummage sale."

"Oh?" Uncle Theodore sounded as if he didn't believe Nick. But then he grumbled, "I guess Wilma could have picked it up by mistake and taken it to the rummage sale."

Steff demanded, "Why didn't you give it to my uncle?"

Nick looked down. "I *thought* it was yours, Mr. Newton. But there was no name in it."

"No name? There should have been a white card on the cover."

"There wasn't. Anyway, I planned to give it to you later."

"After you found the treasure," said Paulie.

"That treasure is mine!" Nick declared. "My Grandmother Beulah gave it to me."

"Your grandmother?" Uncle Theodore exclaimed. "What do you mean?"

"Beulah was my grandmother. The last time I saw her before she died, she told me she had hidden a treasure in the swamp when she was twelve years old. She never came back here. She wanted me to have that treasure."

"Did she tell you where it was?" asked Uncle Theodore.

Nick held up the paper he had been reading. It dripped tea-colored water. "Yes. I drew this map from what she said, but when I got here, I still couldn't find her house. So I tried to learn everything that I could about the people who once lived in the swamp."

Uncle Theodore scowled. "By using your handy-dandy video camera—recording my talks and bothering my nieces."

"I'm sorry," said Nick. "I should have asked first."

"That's right!" Uncle Theodore said.

Nick told Steff and Paulie, "I wasn't taking

video pictures of you at the rummage sale. I knew the paper you found had something to do with Beulah. I zoomed in close with my camera lens, trying to read it."

Steff turned to Uncle Theodore. "How do we know Beulah was his grandmother?"

"Good question," said Russell.

Nick pulled an envelope from his bag. "Here. This is her last letter to me."

Uncle Theodore studied it. "I suppose Beulah could have written this." He read some aloud. " 'Nick, I pray that when you find the treasure, you will understand its value.' " He gave back the letter. "I still can't imagine that little girl having any treasure. Folks around here didn't have much money."

Nick said, "Well, she hid something she wanted me to have. I admit I did follow you people today. But from here, I think I can find Beulah's house. Although my map"—he looked at Steff—"is sopping wet from that tumble I took in the water."

Steff blinked. Nick had said *tumble*. Now she remembered the last two lines of Beulah's poem.

"Come on!" she cried. "I know Beulah's hiding place!"

15

beulah's secret

Steff led the others back to Beulah's home and to the strangely shaped little hill.

They pulled away enough grass and weeds to see that under the dirt was a big pile of metal rails.

"These are pieces of old, rusty railroad track," said Uncle Theodore. "Extra rails must have been dumped here when the railroad was being built."

Steff shot an arm in the air. "Yes! When Nick said he *tumbled* into the water, I remembered the rest of the poem.

The tumbled rails above my face—
They know about my hiding place."

Paulie said, "Tumbled rails. I get it."

Nick protested, "I'm not going to waste time looking at a pile of old rails."

Uncle Theodore said, "Hold on. Steff, let's hear all of Beulah's poem."

She read from her sticky notes and added the last two lines. "Here goes! . . .

My Secret

While taking a dip in a cup of tea,
A glorious treasure came to me.
It waits inside a house of glass
At trail's end where people pass.
A garden grows, a rooster crows,
By cypress knees where trees once rose.
The tumbled rails above my face—
They know about my hiding place."

Uncle Theodore said, "Steff's right. Clues in the poem led us to Beulah's old home. Perhaps these rails do hold the secret to her treasure."

"Let's find a place in the rails big enough to hide something," said Steff.

"Careful," Uncle Theodore said. "We don't want anyone hurt." He began poking a long stick at the rails.

Nick said, "I don't see any house of glass."

Uncle Theodore's stick kept thumping against the hard metal rails until one time it broke through. It slid far inside.

"Aha!" he cried.

They quickly cleared away more dirt and plants and found an open space.

Uncle Theodore pushed and pulled on the rails to see if any would fall.

Russell banged a stick around the inside. "Let's scare out the swamp critters." Then came the sound of breaking glass. "Oops!"

"House of glass!" cried Paulie.

Steff peered inside. "I can't see much."

Nick took a flashlight from his bag and stepped toward the hole.

Uncle Theodore said, "Let Steff look."

Steff shone the flashlight. The beam hit a

shiny spot on the ground.

"There's the broken glass," she said. "I think it was a jar."

She flashed the light above the broken glass. "Yes, I see a place in the rails—like a shelf— where the jar was hidden."

Nick said, "Never mind where it was. What was in it?"

By this time, Steff was on her hands and knees almost inside the hole.

Uncle Theodore warned, "Don't crawl under those rails."

"I can already reach the jar," Steff said.

He tossed his cap to her. "Put everything in here." He grabbed her ankles as if ready to yank her back.

Steff picked up the big pieces of glass. "It had a funny kind of lid."

"Watch for diamonds in that broken glass," said Nick.

Uncle Theodore snorted.

"I found a piece of paper," said Steff.

"Oh no!" Paulie giggled and clapped her hands to her face. "Not a sticky note!"

"Right!" teased Russell. "Like people had sticky notes in the olden days!"

"Could the paper be money?" asked Nick.

"Here's something else." Steff backed out from the rails, bringing her uncle's cap.

Uncle Theodore said, "Aha! The house of glass was a canning jar. See the old-fashioned lid? Jars like this were used for canning vegetables."

Steff held up a small piece of wood for everyone to see. "Here's the treasure that was inside the jar."

"That?" demanded Nick. "I don't believe it!"

"A cross!" Paulie exclaimed. "A cross carved out of wood."

Russell carefully unfolded the piece of paper. He took the flashlight and read, " 'Given to Beulah at her baptism in Teacup Lake.' It's signed 'Pastor Johnson.' " He looked up and said, "There's a lake near here shaped like a teacup."

"Ooh," breathed Steff. "Baptized in Teacup Lake. That explains the poem's first line. 'While taking a dip in a cup of tea.' "

Uncle Theodore cleared his throat. He spoke softly, "To Beulah, this wooden cross was a glorious treasure. It was a gift from her pastor—a memory of her baptism."

Nick mumbled, "I guess Grandmother Beulah's baptism was important to her."

Uncle Theodore nodded. "A person's baptism is always important. It's when we tell everyone that we have promised to follow Jesus."

Steff looked at Nick. "It sounds as if Beulah hoped you would follow Jesus, too."

Paulie told him, "I'm sorry you don't get any diamonds or money. But following Jesus is better than diamonds or money."

Steff expected Nick to argue with that.

Instead, he took the wooden cross. He turned it over and over, and he rubbed his fingers on its smooth edges. He said thoughtfully, "My grandmother used to talk to me about Jesus and the cross. I'm afraid I didn't listen well."

He held the cross out to Steff. "Here, you found this."

She shook her head and tucked her hands behind her back. "Beulah wanted you to have her treasure."

Russell was studying the paper. "Pastor Johnson wrote something else to Beulah. 'Remember Colossians 3:16: "Let the word of Christ dwell in you richly. . . ." ' "

A warm feeling flooded over Steff. "We know that verse, don't we, Paulie? We know all about hiding the Word in our hearts."

Paulie hugged Uncle Theodore. "Using sticky-note reminders, of course."

Steff laughed. "Oh yes! Sticky notes—also good for finding lost notebooks and hidden treasure!"